MW01009040

by **JAN CARR**

illustrated by

DOROTHY DONOHUE

Holiday House / New York

SEP 28 2007

For Regina and Dorothy,
A couple of sweethearts,
And for Charlie and Stan, with love
J. C.

To my *baby* sweethearts,
Henry, Noah, and Super Dave

With special thanks to Holiday House
for making this happen
D. D.

Text copyright © 2003 by Jan Carr
Illustrations copyright © 2003 by Dorothy Donohue
All Rights Reserved
Printed in the United States of America
www.holidayhouse.com

Library of Congress Cataloging-in-Publication Data
Carr, Jan.
Sweet hearts / Jan Carr; illustrated by Dorothy Donohue.—1st ed.
p. cm.
Summary: A young boy celebrates Valentine's Day
by making and hiding paper hearts around the house for his family to discover.
Includes directions for making hearts and a brief history of Valentine's Day.
ISBN 0-8234-1732-8 (hardcover)
ISBN 0-8234-1879-0 (paperback)
[1. Valentine's Day—Fiction.] I. Donohue, Dorothy, ill. II. Title.
PZ8.3.C21683 Sw 2002
[E]—dc21
2001059404

Why Do We Celebrate Valentine's Day?

No one knows for sure how Valentine's Day got started, but we do know that people have celebrated it, or something like it, for a very long time.

In ancient times, the Romans held a festival each year in the middle of February. There, young men would draw the names of girls from a jar, and they would be paired as sweethearts.

Later, Christians, too, adopted February 14 as a day to celebrate love. They named the day after St. Valentine, a priest who may have helped young people in love. It is said that he married couples in secret at a time when the emperor had ordered all young men to go to war, and had forbidden them to get married.

Today, many people celebrate the day by giving valentines to the people they love. Often these cards are shaped like hearts.

Who are the people in your heart? Are you going to make them valentines? Will you surprise them, too?

One heart on the bathroom mirror,
One heart in a shoe,

One heart by my mommy's mug
To tell her "I love you!"

One heart in an envelope—

Mail it far away.

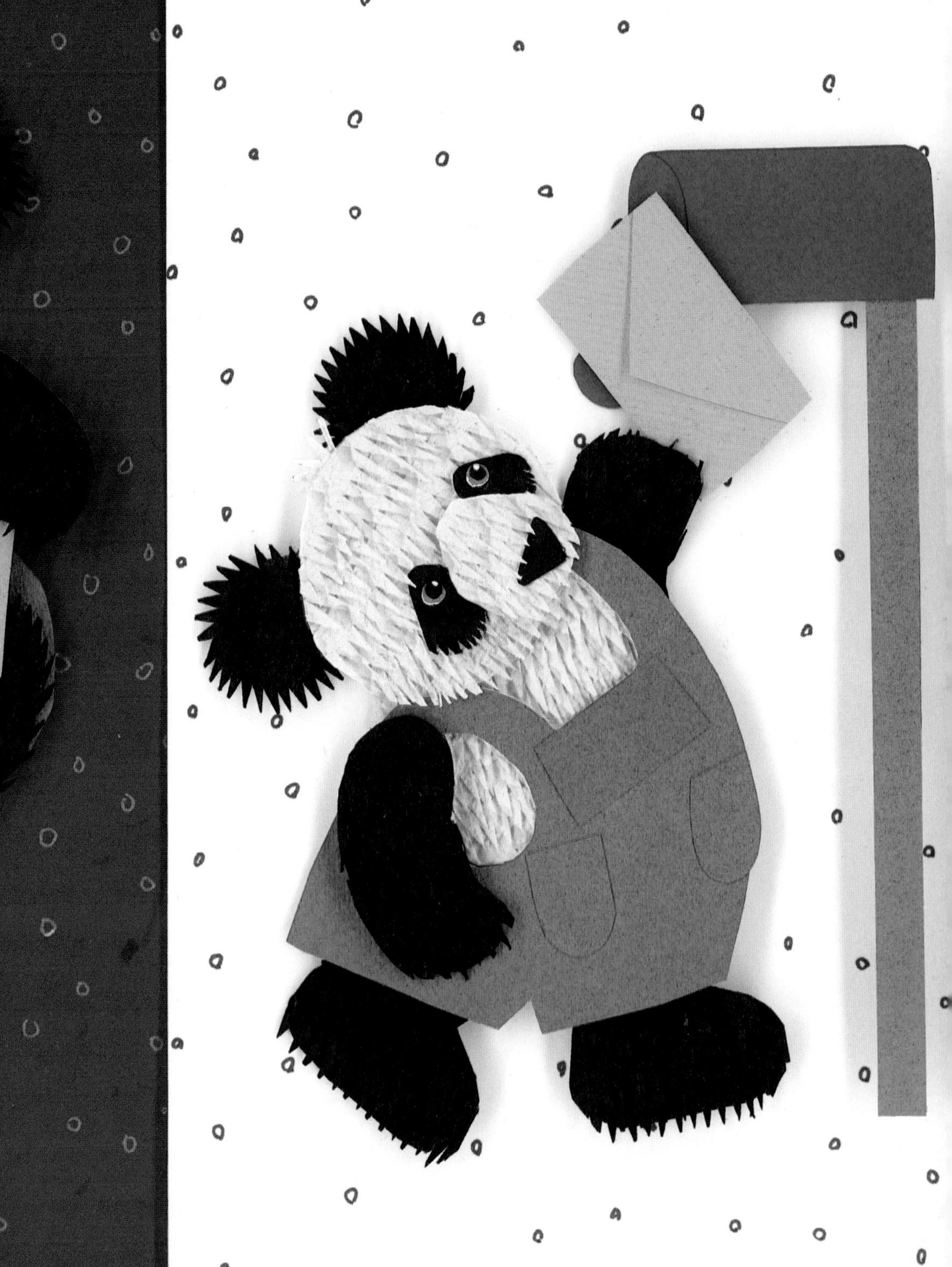

Cut out lots
of valentines.
Hey, look!
A heart bouquet!

Lace and foil
And tissue scraps;
Glitter, ribbon, glue.

Someone's hiding
Heaps of hearts.

Bet you can't guess who!

One heart by the baby's crib,
One set near her plate.

One heart by the doggie's dish—
Don't eat it, Spot! Too late!

One heart tucked inside your sleeve,
Playing heart-and-seek.

Find some more, a pocketful!

Daddy, did you peek?

Daddy finally guesses it.
I fooled him
From the start.

Mommy plants a kiss and tells me
I'm their sweetest heart.

How to Make Hearts

It's fun and simple to make hearts. Here's how.

Get a piece of paper. You might want to use red construction paper.

Fold the paper in half.

Near the fold, draw one half of a heart. The picture shows what the shape should look like, but you can have a grown-up help you draw it if you want.

Cut along the line you drew, making sure to cut out both halves of the folded paper.

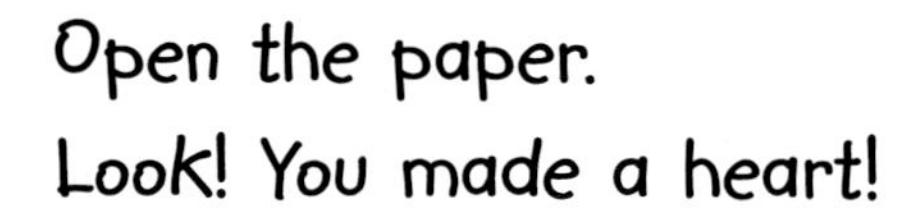

Open the paper.
Look! You made a heart!

You can decorate your heart any way you want. Use crayons, markers, glitter, beads, doilies, buttons, feathers, pieces of ribbon, tin foil—or anything else you can think of!

ISCARDED